Anni Reinhardt
Amelie – unwanted and unloved

Anni Reinhardt

Amelie
unwanted and unloved

Bibliografische Information der
Deutschen Nationalbibliothek:
Die Deutsche Nationalbibliothek verzeichnet diese
Publikation in der Deutschen Nationalbibliografie;
detaillierte bibliografische Daten sind im Internet unter
www.dnb.de abrufbar.

English translation and editing: Angela Hoffmann
www.Angela-Hoffmann.com

Legal advice:
RA Meinrad Mayer, Frankfurt am Main

Creative consulting:
Angela Hoffmann & Klaus Grelewicz

Designed by DigiBuchService, Hannover
www.digibuchservice.de

Production and Published by:
BoD – Books on Demand, Norderstedt

Cover picture
Front: Pixabay #1821187
Back: Pixabay #3112378

ISBN: 978-3-7448-9607-8

After a hard day's work in October 1941, the farmer's family sat on the oak bench in front of their straw-covered house. All the family members were happy to have managed the hard work in this godforsaken area of Slovenia, the last corner of Lower Styria on the border with Croatia. The farmer, a former soldier on horseback in the First World War, was of medium height and had thinning hair. His very slender wife wore her hair, already streaked with silver threads, braided into a plait. Their two sons were named Anton and Franz. Anton, the elder, was later to take over the farm. Franz flirted with a profession in uniform. The 16-year-old daughter, father's favourite, was always at the top of her class and wanted to go to secondary school. She was her father's pride. She was a pretty young girl with beautiful thick black hair and brown eyes.

The harvest that year was good. The granaries were full and the cattle healthy in the stables. Full barrels of red wine were stored in the vineyard. They tasted the wine for the first time that evening. "It will be good, but it still has to mature for some

5

time," the farmer announced. It was getting late that evening when a beautiful sunset red appeared in the sky. An evening glow predicts good weather for the next day, which they could well use. But the farmer's wife cried out: "Don't rejoice. The sunset red is blood red, there will be war." And she was right. They had no radio and no newspaper. They orientated themselves on nature and its change in the cycle of the year. A week later Hitler annexed Slovenia. Lower Styria was a thorn in his side.

So the order was given that all the inhabitants of this region had to assemble at a certain place within a week. Everyone was allowed to take what they could carry. Crying and complaining, swearing and cursing could be heard everywhere during the following days. A whole year's work was in vain. The cattle had to be sold quickly to Croatia so that the animals could continue to live. The news that Hitler had already ordered foreign settlers into the area became a sad certainty. They, too, had to leave their homes and their belongings. The farmer's wife packed her bags with her daughter. The sons took care of the farm with their father. She only had to put together the most necessary things for each of them individually that would fit into the suitcases. She wrapped the wooden carved cross from the corner of the Lord's God in a towel and placed it carefully under the laundry in her brown leather suitcase. The daughter went to help her while the mother-in-law, beyond 75, sat on the wooden bench by the brown tiled stove and wept bitterly. Now everyone left their houses and went to the meeting place. Many people were already there and did not know where the journey was going.

After about 10 kilometres they reached the station. They were exhausted from the long march on the gravel road. The old people and the small children had been put on the oxcarts. The forests they marched past already wore their bright colours and were shone on by the autumn sun. The long train was already waiting for them. Some people from the Sava area had already taken their places. It was not a passenger train, but open waggons in which cattle were usually transported. They were padded with straw and the people were loaded in like animals. The night was cold, but leaving home was more painful. They drove all night and reached the railway station in Aulendorf in Baden-Württemberg the other afternoon. They all had to get off the train.

Hungry and exhausted, they were now herded into the Saint Johan Blönried monastery. Here the families were separated. The men remained here in the camp until further notice. They were assigned to certain jobs. They were also medically examined, measured and weighed. If they met the Führer's required measurements, they were lucky. So the farmer got a job as a stoker on the steam locomotive. His two sons had to go to Russia as soldiers in the Wehrmacht and never came back. In the cemetery chapel in Aulendorf, their names can be read on the plaque of the fallen. One relative was a butcher and was urgently needed in this camp. He did not have to suffer hunger like so many others. The women came with their children to the convent of Sießen near Saulgau, which was also converted into a camp. Most of the nuns were expelled by the SS leadership. Some were allowed to stay. The large crowd of expellees was housed and bedded on straw sacks. They, too, were measured, medically examined and sorted out. For example, the farmer's mother-in-law was sent to the Neresheim convent, which had also been converted into a camp. She soon died and never saw her family again.

Life in the camp was not easy for the displaced persons. Everything was foreign to them. The young people did not speak a word of German, but the old people spoke it very well.

Before the First World War, German was the official language in Lower Styria. The farmer's daughter came to Aulendorf as a domestic helper in an inn. The owner, the wife of an SA officer, took her in. She first taught her the language by taking each object in her hand and naming it or explaining it to her. The young woman learned quickly and was gradually entrusted with bigger tasks. Home was far away, but at least she could see her beloved father more often.

Slowly the camp cleared. The young boys came to the farmers to help the women because their sons and husbands were at the front. Some never came home again. At first the strangers were met with suspicion, but over time things smoothed out and people were glad to have capable helpers. One young man called Hans, at the age of 18, came to a family where the sons and the father were serving as soldiers in the German army. He was lucky as he had been used to farm work since childhood. He was tall and slim and even resembled one of the sons. On Sunday afternoons he was allowed to visit his mother and siblings in the Sießen camp. The farmer's wife gave him all kinds of food. Hunger was the biggest enemy in the camp. Years later he told about it again and again.

The war became more and more cruel, the people more and more despondent. Faith in God gave them strength and stamina. Night after night, the farmer's wife took her cross out of her suitcase and prayed the rosary with her roommates. Praying gave her strength and support. She was firmly convinced that one day they would be heard. It took another four long years until the war ended in May 1945.

Summer had come. The sun heated up mightily at the end of June. To wash themselves, the camp inmates had to fetch water from the farm well with a zinc bucket. So the farmer's wife had her daughter, who was already back in the camp, fetch water late in the evening. The day was long over and night was not far away. She filled the water bucket to the brim when she was suddenly held by a strong man's hand. At gunpoint, the SS officer forced her behind the monastery wall, tore off her beautiful, colourful summer dress and went to town on her. "If you scream now, I'll shoot you!" he said. He also punched her in the face, so hard that blood dripped from her injured lip. "Finally I have achieved what I had planned for a long time," the SS man said and hit her so hard that she lost consciousness for a short time. The perpetrator disappeared into the darkness. When she slowly regained consciousness and tried to sit up, her whole body ached. Half-naked and covered in blood, she staggered in the darkness towards Wagenhauser Weiher, where she was later found by the search party. She did not want to go back to the camp. She wanted to end her young life here in the lake. She jumped into the lake in front of everyone. A young man jumped in and saved her. He took off his shirt, covered her bruised body and brought her back to the camp. It was agreed that nothing would be said about what had happened.

The Slovenians were now free to decide whether they wanted to go back to their homeland or build a new future here. They all wanted to go back. Here they would be strangers among strangers.

Exactly four years after the expulsion, there was great excitement in the monastery. Finally the time had come. Packed full, they waited to be taken away. Families moved together, helping each other. But some had died. The young woman stood with her family with the man who had saved her from drowning. The farmer's wife did not like the connection because Hans came from a poor background. His father was a railway worker and a farmer on the side, his mother an efficient housewife.

They returned the same way they had come. A thousand questions now arose. How will they find their properties? How will they survive the coming winter? The weather suited them that October. But it would get colder soon.

Back at the farm, they did not know whether to cry or to scream. The settlers had left chaos in their absence. The granaries were almost empty. There were no cattle in the barn and rain dripped through the thatched roof right into the parlour. The farmer, by now suffering from asthma, did not let himself be put off. "We survived the war. We can manage this, too." Together they made a plan. "Hans, you go to the farmers in Croatia and try to find our cattle. Buy another pig." He said to the women: "You go to our fields and look for turnips and potatoes. The settlers didn't expect us to come home and there must be plenty left to harvest." "And what are you doing in the meantime, father?" asked the daughter. "I'm going to the vineyard to see what's going on." With these words he took the wine cellar key from the hook and also took the woven

15

wine basket and, leaning on the stick, went into his beloved vineyard.

To his delight, there were still many red grapes hanging on the vines, waiting to be harvested. Even in the big 10-hectolitre barrel there was still the rest of the last years. He filled the 5-litre bottle with the red juice, locked the cellar and went home. Hans brought home a cow and a pig weighing about 50 kilograms. The women found a few rows of potatoes and fodder beet. Also bean poles with dry pods, plus some pumpkins. They brought home what they could carry.

The weather gods were kind to them over the next few weeks. Former helpers from Croatian mountains also came to their aid. They brought along feathered fowl and eggs. They wanted to thank them for the time before the war when they had received help on the farm. From a miller they got a sack of wheat flour and a sack of maize flour. In their forest they raked the dry leaves and brought them home in back baskets. It served as a base for the animals in winter. They had harvested everything and even pressed some wine. There was plenty of milk. What they could spare during the day, the farmer's wife poured into earthen vessels. Soon a thick layer of cream formed, and underneath was sour milk. The cream was scooped into a butter churn and churned into butter, then washed in cold water and shaped. It tasted delicious with a slice of fresh corn bread and sour milk. The remaining sour milk was made into curd on the cooker at a mild temperature. The white cabbage heads from the garden were cut and made into sauerkraut. By the end of October everything was done.

The consequences of that terrible night became more visible from day to day. The two young people dressed festively and had themselves married in church. From now on, Hans called his wife Tina. Christmas was just around the corner. Hans fetched a small spruce tree from the forest, fitted it into a wooden stand and placed it in the corner under the cross. Mother and daughter decorated the tree with apples, sweets and cotton wool. Mulled wine diluted with well water and a few crackling biscuits, sour milk and fresh maize bread was a delicacy for them on Christmas Eve after four years in a foreign country. At midnight, the whole community gathered in the parish church. They were happy to be able to sing Christmas carols in their mother tongue again after years. They did not feel any cold, they were just happy and grateful to have survived the terrible war and the expulsion. The farmer's wife's brother, the butcher, was called all over the area for home slaughtering. He always brought his sister meat and bacon. So they had lard to cook with and some meat to eat.

Mother and daughter sat in the warm parlour on cold winter days and sewed baby clothes. Everything was handmade. There was nothing to buy at that time. Finally the weather changed. The sun melted the snow with its warm rays. On the hills, the first signs of spring rose from the earth. Early in the morning, the birds trilled, chased each other and built their nests. There was no doubt that spring was just around the corner. The daughter had gone into labour pains. The midwife, a sister of the mother, was hurriedly sent for.

"It's going to take a while," she said, "the cervix isn't open enough yet." The woman in labour cried out in pain, but she had to bear it. Once again, endure it all. Hans was with her, wiped the sweat from her forehead, comforting her. Towards evening, one contraction after another came. The midwife shouted: "You have to push, Tina, it will be over soon." Already the little head was coming, the shoulders, finally, a girl. The midwife cut the umbilical cord. The child screamed. For a brief moment, the young mother lost consciousness. She was completely exhausted from the long birth. The midwife wanted to give the child into her arms, but she refused. "No, I don't want the child, never wanted it." Whatever had happened, it was not the child's fault. It was healthy, had all its limbs and was quite lively. While the midwife was bathing, weighing and measuring the child, the body of the woman in labour got rid of the afterbirth. Then she was washed and given pads. The little creature was now hungry, but the mother would not let it touch her breast. After much toing and froing, the midwife put the baby on, to no avail. No milk flow. Now Hans held the child in his arms, quite awkwardly, he didn't know what to do with it. The midwife now prepared the bottle, took the child in her arms and let it drink. "What should the child be called?" she continued to ask. The new grandmother entered the room and said: "Amelie should be her name." Then she put the child into the prepared basket, where it immediately fell asleep.

Now her attention turned to the mother, who was still crying. Hans brought her warm chicken broth, but she would not drink anything, pushing him away. "I just want to die. So many women die in childbed. Why do I have to live? I never wanted this, it was forced on me." Now a light came on for the midwife. "Was she, too?" Hans nodded. "It's no use, Tina, you have to get up and to walk a few steps. Otherwise, there is a danger of thrombosis and embolism." Supported by Hans and the midwife, she walked to the window and back again. As she did so, she looked at the sleeping child. "You are a mother, you have responsibility, no matter how it came about. My work for today is finished. Tomorrow I will be back." Hans accompanied the midwife and told her about that night in the camp. Slowly, the young mother recovered; she did not have much time for it for there was a lot of work on the farm.

Early in the morning of the feast of the Ascension, the godmother Mary came from the city to carry the child to the Chapel of the Cross for baptism. The child was dressed nicely, laid in a pillow and covered with a lace blanket. Except for grandfather, who was once again plagued by severe asthma, everyone accompanied the child as if in procession. They walked the steep path through the vineyards and were accompanied by the morning sun. Cornelian cherries with yellow blossoms and sweet cherries with white blossoms greeted them on the hills. At the wine cellar, apricots stretched their pink blossoms towards the insects. On the willow catkin, hungry bees cavorted. Wagtails also strutted through the fresh greenery. The ringing of the bells of the Chapel of the Cross could be heard far down into the valley. The faithful came from all over to attend the service that is celebrated here every year on this day. The altar was hewn from stone and stood close to the wooden cross, which reached up to the ceiling with its longitudinal beam. There were no seats, only a few chairs today for the baptismal community. The floor was covered with stones and smoothed out with mortar. Everyone who climbs to this chapel enjoys the magnificent view of the Croatian mountains. In good weather, you can even see as far as Marburg on the Drava. To the east, on the other hand, the view expands over the entire Sattelbach Valley. For the first year after their return, the people were happy and grateful to be reunited here. At the end of the solemn service, the child was baptised with the name Amelie. She had been asleep during the whole ceremony. The cross became her life support, a straw to which she would continually hold on.

Life was hard. There was endless work on the farm but few helping hands. To make matters worse, Hans had to serve in the army in Osijek for a few months. Farmers helped each other. They ploughed, harrowed and sowed. The women planted potatoes in the rows and sowed all kinds of vegetables. The vineyard also called for workers. The freshly cut vines had to be tied up so that the wind would not break the canes. Tina fell into bed dead tired in the evening. Grandmother was no different. Fortunately, Amelie slept through the whole night and during the day she was in good hands with grandfather. He was also the only one who loved the child. After one and a half years, she had a baby brother who was very much loved by the mother. The two children grew up, were put to work and stuck together like peanuts. Grandfather told them stories about the war, legends about the saints and in the evenings he explained the firmament to them. There was no radio nor newspaper, and nature told you what the weather would be like tomorrow. The dew in the morning predicted a beautiful day, but when the grass was dry, the rain was not far away.

Amelie started school at the age of 6. It was a bad day for the frightened girl.

Everything was strange to her. Nobody knew her. The teacher put her in the second row next to Tilli, a girl who had to walk 5 kilometres to school every day. Bread was scarce at home, but she had an apple with her for the break, which she traded with Amelie for a piece of cornbread. For the primary school pupils, lessons began at 12:30 p.m. and lasted until 5:00 p.m. Amelie had big problems with the ABC. She could not form the letters into a word. "What did I do to deserve having such a stupid child?" her mother shouted at her and slapped her on the fingers. She took refuge with her grandfather, who explained letter by letter, and she learned to spell. Over time, school became her friend, otherwise she was not allowed to have one. Before school and again in the evenings, she had to help around the house: fill up wood for the next day, fetch water from the community well and look after the feathered fowl. There was no time to play.

As she grew older, the pigsty was also her territory. Her brother, on the other hand, had to work in the big stable. He did not make friends at school. He copied his homework from his sister. Both were bound by deep brotherly love and both feared their strict father, who punished them for every little thing. They had to kneel on the grains or were beaten over the back with the rod. The two had to be enough for each other because they were not allowed to have friends.

They helped with the hay harvest by pounding the hay in the hayloft. A rusty nail stuck out of the old planks and Amelie, of all people, stepped into it. She lifted her foot, freed herself from the evil and continued working. During the night, she got severe pain in the front of her foot and could not walk. She finally dared to report that she was in pain. "Can't you be careful? That's what you get now. Too stupid for everything," the mother continued to scold her. After the second night, the pain was unbearable. She got a high fever, the forefoot around the little toe was red and swollen. A small red line moved towards the knee. On the carrier, the mother took her to the local doctor's surgery. He just took one look at the feverish girl and her foot, glanced at his wristwatch and said: "To the hospital, immediately! In ten minutes the bus leaves for the nearby town. Here you have my referral. Hurry up. It looks like blood poisoning." During the 25-kilometre journey, the mother did not speak a word to her. She was just angry that she had to go to the hospital in the midst of all her work.

Since Amelie could neither eat nor drink anything all day, she immediately ended up on the operating table. Under a short ether anaesthetic, a decompression incision was made under the little toe so that pus could drain away. She had to stay in hospital overnight, but her mother was sent home as soon as she arrived. "You were lucky, my child, one day later you would have been singing with the angels." "That would have been nice, doctor", Amelie responded.

Later that day she was brought home by her uncle on his motorbike. Before that, he bought her a new school bag, which she was allowed to choose herself, and notebooks and pens to go with it. She was still weak and had pain in her foot, but she was immediately driven to work. Mother reproached her for how much she had cost again.

The summer holidays began in June so that the children could help with the farming. Many were looking forward to the holidays, but Amelie would have preferred to stay at school. The summer was hot and humid. The wheat harvest began as early as July. They got up early at 2 o'clock in the morning. With the scythe, father mowed the golden-yellow ripe grain, row by row. The Mother and the children, sometimes even the grandmother, gathered it and tied sheaves. At noon, the sun heated up powerfully, so much so that everything living sought the shade. The family rested. In the late afternoon, they collected the sheaves with the ox cart and spread them out to dry between wooden beams at home. As soon as the whole crop had been mown and stored and dried at home, the threshing began.

The neighbours were happy to help each other because on such days there was something particularly good to eat. No sooner had the fruit been taken care of than maize, turnips, runner beans and pumpkins still had to be chopped. The cabbage plants also needed fertiliser and water. The children were tired and couldn't take it anymore, but they were not allowed to rest. They had to keep working. Life was hard and demanding. They knew nothing but work.

"Oh, how nice it would be at school now," Amelie thought while drawing water from the community well in the evening. "Even though it's the holidays, I don't have any time to read." The only joy now in August were the first ripe grapes in the vineyard. They were followed by juicy apricots and peaches. Going to Sunday service in the parish church was a matter of course for Amelie. Her brother, however, preferred to play football at that hour. On the way home, she explained the sermon to him, which her father always wanted to know. It was a kind of test to see if they had really been in church for he himself stayed away. The summer was drawing to a close, the second cut of grass was already under the roof. Finally, in mid-September, school started and Amelie entered form 5. New subjects were added to the timetable. The first foreign language — German —, history, geography, Slovenian, mathematics and sports. Too bad that classes started at 7:30 a.m. since she still had to deliver milk to the dairy at 7:00 a.m. After that, she had to walk 2 kilometres to school in a hurry. She wanted to arrive on time, but she didn't always succeed. She would have liked to take part in the English class, but since it started at 7:00 a.m., this was out of the question.

The time for the way home was prescribed. She had to get home as quickly as possible so that she could get some things done in the field. She had no time to study. So she got up every morning at 4 o'clock, made a fire in the cooker so that she had warm water to wash. Then she did her homework and studied by heart. While washing dishes on Sunday, she hurt her middle finger on a knife. She wiped off the dripping blood and paid no further attention until the finger swelled up and hurt excruciatingly. The father took a razor blade and scratched the wound, not knowing what the consequences of his actions would be. The whole middle hand hurt so much that she could no longer even write. "You're just too stupid, you can't even do the dishes," her mother scolded. Amelie kept silent. She felt like screaming from pain, but all she did was crying.

Fortunately, the school doctor came to examine her. He held out his hand to greet her. Amelie refused him hers. "What's wrong, child?" he asked with a worried expression. She showed him her hand. "Does it hurt very much?" he asked caringly. "Is your mother with you?" „Yes." „As soon as I have finished here, you come with your mother to the surgery. The finger has to be cut open, there's no other way," the medical officer said.

Amelie paced back and forth in the hallway, waiting for her mother. "We're going home," she cried. "No, mother, the finger has to be cut open." Immediately the nurse called her. The mother had to go, too. They put the girl on a chair, gave her a glass of wine to drink, as an anaesthetic, so to speak. The doctor had not expected such an intervention. He saw it as his duty to help the child. The mother had to hold the daughter's arm while the nurse disinfected the hand with iodine. With a scalpel, he cut the middle finger at the side and in the middle so that the pus could drain away. The girl only cried out when the doctor pushed the tamponade through the opening. She was then given a tight bandage and dressing material to take home. "Take better care of your child," he admonished the mother. The only important thing was that there was no charge in the process. The nurse gave further instructions for changing the bandage and told her to bathe the finger in lukewarm camomile tea. Amelie was still a bit dizzy from the wine and slowly groped after her mother, but that woman only had scolding words for her. She only cared about the labour and not about her daughter's health. Sure, every helping hand was needed on a farm, there was always a lot to do.

At the end of the school year, each class had to cover 1 kilometre in a rush. The first ones would get a prize. After the class had covered half the distance, Amelie collapsed, gasping for breath. "Come on girls, otherwise we'll never get the prize." Amelie just wasn't able to get up. Coughing and struggling for breath, she remained sitting on the side of the road. No one was interested in her, there was just a "C" on her report card for sports.

Later in adulthood, she was diagnosed with a defect in the pulmonary valve, which was congenital. It did not cause her any problems in normal everyday life, but at great exertion she experienced shortness of breath because the valve did not close completely and the blood that supplied the lungs flowed back then. She was classified as a student who did not want to exert herself and was too lazy to walk.

In the 6th academic year, botany and biology were added to the existing subjects. The worst thing now was that Latin names had to be learnt for every flower and plant. "How on earth shall I read five more books over the year and even recite them?" she thought with concern. On cool days, sports took place in the gym. Everyone had to line up and then, one by one, jump over the trestle covered in brown leather. During the jump, the girl's top slipped up, revealing the welts on her back. The teacher screwed up her face but didn't say a word about it.

Beech logs had been lying in the wood yard for days, waiting to be sawn. It was a sunny October day. "Let's grasp the opportunity straightaway," the father said, hoisting the logs onto a wooden trestle and sharpening the 2-metre-long handsaw. "You will help me to saw the wood today, Amelie." "But father, I have to study and read another book." He shouted at her, "I'll get the book-reading out of you yet, you're here to work."

They pulled the saw back and forth. One block of wood after another fell to the ground. "Father, I can't go on, my arms are hurting." He had no sympathy and put on a new log. "Pull!" he shouted. She wailed and cried. He was furious, cut a thorny rod and hit her with it on her thin thighs, so hard that the blood dripped down to her ankles. She screamed so loudly in pain and fear that the grandfather in the parlour heard her crying. Leaning on his stick, he approached Hans, threatened him with his stick and shouted, "Aren't you ashamed to treat the child like that?" "I'll beat the book-reading out of her!" he shouted back. The mother stood at the front door and allowed her child to be abused like this. The grandmother cared for Amelie, washed off her blood, tore old linen and bandaged her legs. She dried her tears and comforted her. In time, the wounds on her legs healed, but her soul remained deeply wounded and she was very doleful.

Her mother didn't care of what was happening and never said a word about it. Amelie was not allowed to read her books but had to go to work in the fields instead. She was too stupid to give an abridged version. The mother stayed at home, read the books and wrote summaries, which Amelie had to copy out then.

In the last classes she was given chemistry, which she loved very much, but she didn't like physics at all. "That's something for boys," she used to say, "uninteresting for us girls."

She finished secondary school with school grade 4, which was second best at that time. She was very sorry that her school days were over. She would have liked to continue school in the district town, but no one would pay for the costs.

She approached the magistrate at the town hall. "Maybe he can help me?" "I'm sure something can be arranged," said the tall gentleman with his full, greying hair at the temples. "You'll have to cancel your church, it is all lies anyway, and get our red badge." "No," Amelie objected. "I don't want to become a communist." "Then you'll continue to be a maid on your farm." She turned around and wordlessly left the office, letting the door fall into the lock behind her.

On the way home she wrestled with herself, cried out to God and doubted herself. There was no help in sight. Then she remembered the story of her pastor: "A man complains to God that He had promised to always be with him, but in the sand he sees only *one* trace. 'Where have you been, God, when I needed you most?' 'My child,' says God, 'I carried you.'" "Do you carry me, too?" Amelie asked, her eyes fixed on the sky. "I entirely rely on You. Show me the way, please."

She had grown into a pretty young woman by now. Her hair was chestnut brown and she had blue eyes. What would her future look like? "It's four more years until I come of age, until I have to endure all this here." No matter what Amelie did, her mother would always be malcontent, insulting and humiliating her. On Saturdays, Amelie scrubbed the kitchen floor, kneeling down. Father was in a fury once again. With great force, he knocked over the full cleaning bucket and shouted at her: "I'll teach you how to clean."

Grandmother kept in close contact with the grande dame, the owner of an inn in Aulendorf during the war. With Amelie, she only spoke German, which Amelie mastered fluently. After all, German was spoken and written in the old script here during the time of the k.u.k. Monarchy.

One Sunday afternoon, the question came up as to who would or should take over the farm one day. "I would like to take it over," Amelie said. Her mother faced her and responded, "You won't! Your brother will take it over." What needs to be mentioned: The farm was her mother's property, so her father had no say in this matter. Now Amelie knew that she had to go away — far away. Her grandparents supported her decision. As soon as she would be of age, she wanted to get a passport with a tourist visa, and then she wanted to go away — far away. The mere thought of this made her feel better. The pastor of the parish also supported her concerning her plan as he knew about the situation, but he had to keep quiet.

All day long she toiled in the fields or in the vineyard, the fear of her father constantly accompanying her. When she was 13, she had to bake an apple strudel in a wood and coal cooker. She had no experience of how to fire the stove with beech wood. Consequently, the oven got too much heat and the strudel got a dark colour. For this, her father slapped her on her bare bottom and later she had to eat what was burnt.

At last the time had come. She was of age. Just the thought of finally freeing herself made her heart beat faster. Grandmother had already fetched her brown little suitcase with silver fittings. Amelie had little to pack. A dress, a skirt, a blouse, a waistcoat and some underwear. In addition, grandmother had prepared a handbag for her with her lace handkerchief. Grandfather gave her his savings. "Here you are," he said, "it's not much and I won't need it anymore."

Everything was ready. She just had to wait for the right time. She did not want to leave without saying goodbye to her priest. After the early Mass, she said goodbye. He gave her a silver rosary set with rubies. "So you will not forget what I have taught you when you are in a foreign land." She knelt down and he blessed her. They both wept. Letters would travel back and forth until his death.

The parents had business in town and would not be home until evening. The opportunity was favourable. The brother, who wished her good luck, embraced her dearly. The grandmother had already announced her arrival in Aulendorf and the grandfather hugged her tightly once more. "Farewell, my child, we will not see each other again!" he said softly. "My lungs don't want any more. Be happy, don't forget us." "Yes, grandfather, I promise." "Now, when you walk on the footbridge over the saddle stream, throw all the suffering you have endured here into the water so that you can finally be you and be free."

She had only a few minutes to reach the station, where the steaming locomotive with its waggons was already waiting. One last look at the vineyards and the Chapel of the Cross. How much she had longed for this moment to finally leave, far away! Leaving the beautiful landscape, not knowing what awaited her in a foreign land, made her sad. No, there was no turning back. The train with the puffing, steaming locomotive was already moving towards Zagreb.

Cows grazed in the Sattelbach valley and the cornfields shone in the midday sun The Eagle Mountains with their castle ruins were majestic as ever, greeting Amelie for the last time. After a two-hour journey the train stopped in Zagreb, where the train to Munich was waiting on Platform 1. A ticket was quickly bought and a seat was found. Only now did the hungry stomach make itself known. Grandmother had made provisions. Neatly wrapped in a cloth napkin, she found bread, salami, fruit and a bottle of water.

Slowly, the train left the main station in the direction of Austria. At the border, the locomotive was changed. Customs officers entered the compartment, checked identity papers and asked for dutiable items. Slowly, the train moved on. In Salzburg, the customs officers checked again. Finally they reached Munich.

Amelie got off the train. She was completely overwhelmed by the new surroundings; at the same time, the many people scared her. Where did she have to go now? She showed her ticket to a conductor who was having a coffee and asked him for help. He showed her the train to Ulm, which was already waiting. "In Ulm you have to change trains again to Aulendorf. You will arrive at Platform 2. Your train to Aulendorf is already waiting on the platform opposite."

She arrived there around noon. She took her notebook out of her worn handbag, looking for the drawing her grandmother had made to show her the way to the old lady's inn. Her heart was pounding wildly, but she was brave. She pressed the bell button and waited. She had no idea of the old lady.

The well-groomed old lady with dark hair, in which a few grey threads showed, opened. "Good afternoon!" Amelie said in a weak voice. "You must be Amelie, you are just as beautiful as your mother was then, only a little taller. Your grandmother announced you, asking me to help you." "Will you help me, madam?" "Please don't call me madam, child, I am a simple former innkeeper, nothing else. My husband was a personage at the time of the war. He passed away years ago. Yes, I will help you. I have already arranged things. I have pulled some strings. You must be hungry and tired from the long journey. I didn't think you had such a good command of the German language." "This is grandmother's idea. We practised a lot so that I was the best in German at school." "After you've eaten and rested a little, we'll talk more. I have prepared the guest room for you. You can rest here as long as you like."

Indeed, Amelie was overtired from the long drive. Thoughts of home would not leave her alone. Sure, they would miss the work force, but they would not miss her as a person.

Amelie was right. When her parents got home in the evening, they wondered. There was no fire in the cooker, no water supply and no wood in the box. They called for Amelie, but no one answered. "She's gone," her brother told them, "far away, forever. Next week I'm leaving, too. The draft notice came today, I have to join the soldiers. As soon as my military service is over, I'll be going far away, too." "You can't do that to us, you have to take over the farm," the mother said to him. "I won't, I don't enjoy farming, and even if I did, I wouldn't be allowed to change anything. Amelie, on the other hand, loved farming, she loved every flower, every plant and every tree. She dreamed of making something beautiful out of this estate, but you treated her like a slave. Now she is gone, never to return." "But what will become of us?" the mother asked. "You should have thought about that earlier. It's too late now," he responded.

Amelie had fallen asleep on the nice soft bed. The old lady was waiting with supper in her small dining room, which was furnished with antique furniture. Then, as they sat together, Amelie talked about home, but she did not waste any word on what had happened. But the old lady was well-informed by Amelie's grandmother, she didn't let on, though. "Don't be afraid, everything will be all right. Tomorrow we'll go to the factory owner's family here in town. They need someone for the household. I told them about you, they are looking forward to seeing you. It's a big family: the founder of the company, his wife, both around 80, the daughter with her husband and three growing children. You'll have your own room, a monthly salary and you'll be insured." "How is that supposed to work?" Amelie asked worriedly. "I don't have any working papers yet." "Don't worry, I've thought of everything."

No sooner said than done. Amelie was welcomed like another member of the family. The children took her into their midst and showed her around the villa.

She was allowed to eat at their table and help herself from the soup tureen. In the evenings, she helped the daughter to look after her elderly parents. They enjoyed the loving treatment of the foreign helper and were grateful for the foot baths every evening. Only the language was a problem. Swabian words were not in Amelie's dictionary. She had to ask again and again, but she learned quickly. She also got her documents and was allowed to stay and work for a year. She only wrote home to tell that she was doing well. On Sundays she accompanied the young people to church services, amazed by the beauty of the baroque church. She took great pleasure in housework, always learning something new.

Sunday afternoon was her day off. At lunch, the master of the house wanted to know what she planned to do with her afternoon off. "I want to take the train to Saulgau today and then visit Sießen Abbey." "But you're not going to the monastery, are you?" "No, I just want to see the place where my parents, my grandparents and some relatives spent the

war years. Some of them didn't survive."
"We can go there together," the host suggested. "Thank you, that's very kind of you, but today I'd like to go alone."

She got off the train in Saulgau without having any idea where Sießen Abbey was. So she asked passers-by for directions until she finally spotted the road sign "Sießener Weg" at the hospital, which took her to the monastery. It had been exactly twenty-one years since that October when the Slovenians were allowed to leave the camp and return to their homeland.

Chestnut trees shone with their colourful leaves in front of the entrance gate. Her heart raced, she breathed heavily. A blackbird flew by very close. "The bird is not afraid, it easily finds its nest, and what about me? What do I actually hope to find here?" She strode through the great arch of the monastery grounds, overwhelmed by the beauty spread out before her eyes. She could not believe that such terrible and inhuman things had happened here years ago. The autumn sun's rays made the grounds glow in glorious colours.

She was now looking for the well of which she had been told so much. A Franciscan nun came along the way. She greeted her very kindly. "Can I help you? Are you looking for someone, my dear?" "Yes," replied Amelie, "I think so. During the war there was a camp here where many Slovenians involuntarily spent four years of their existence." "I'm very sorry, that was before my time." "Are there any records of it?" Amelie wanted to know. "Unfortunately not. When the French invaded, the occupiers destroyed everything completely. Why are you interested in that?" the nun wanted to know. "I am the daughter of a Slovenian woman to whom something bad must have happened here. I am simply looking for the truth. Exactly twenty years ago, on a sunny October day, just like today, the Slovenians living here in the camp were allowed to return to their homeland."

Finally, she discovered the well. It looked exactly like the one in the stories. "It's so beautiful and peaceful here today that you simply feel like leaving all your cares behind." She sat down on the wooden bench next to the fountain. "Come again then," the nun said to her. "Yes, that would be nice. But I am just a poor young woman, I have nothing and I am nothing. Fortunately, I have employment with a lovely family." Her glance at her wristwatch revealed it was high time, the train would not wait for her.

Nevertheless, she was back in time for supper. The householder wanted to know whether she had got any of the information she had been looking for. "Unfortunately not," she replied. "And why not?" "There is nothing in the archives from that period from 1941 to 1945, everything was destroyed." "And what did you think you would find?" the landlord continued. "I don't know exactly myself. Perhaps my identity."

She only drank a cup of tea, she couldn't eat anything. Sadness settled around her heart. Tears rolled down her pale cheeks and she did not even know why. At prayer, she came to rest a little, being grateful to be with this friendly family. She learned a lot, and she learned quickly. Swabian cooking, frugal housekeeping, looking after the old parents and keeping the villa in order. The children liked her, no question, she was like their big sister.

At the town festival, she accompanied the youngsters to the fairground in the afternoon. They wanted to dance with their school friends. Amelie sat down on a bench facing the dance floor. Lost in thought, apple juice spritzer in hand, she sat alone at the long table. A man in his 30s approached her and asked her to dance. "Thank you," she said, "I can't dance. I am the young people's escort." "May I sit with you at least?" "Sure, there's plenty of room." He held out his right hand to her. "My name is Hermann," he said. "And you? What's your name?" "Amelie." "You're not from here?" "No," she replied, "I am from far away." Glancing at his wristwatch, he was reminded to go home. "Oh dear, it's already so late. My cows need milking and they're hungry at this time of night." "I know," Amelie said sympathetically. "I come from a farm, too." "Will I see you again?" "If by chance," she replied kindly.

"Who was that?" asked one of the children. "It smells like a stable." "You mean it stinks. It's farm perfume, I think," Amelie continued, "it was a farmer who has to look after his cows so that we always have enough milk, plus cheese and butter and some other things." "Do you know him?" asked one of the children. "No, I've never seen him before."

That late afternoon, Hermann came home as if changed. "What's wrong with you?" his mother, with whom he lived alone, asked. „You are so cheerful today." "I met a young woman today," he said as he changed clothes for work in the stable. "I can't get her out of my mind. I must see her again."

Amelie had long forgotten the encounter with Hermann. She felt well taken care of by the family, yet she was sad. Despite the hard things she had experienced at home, she did not let the connection break. She wrote on holidays, sent congratulations on birthdays, but she received no reply. "They have forgotten me," she thought. Not even on her birthday did she get a few lines. "You shall honour your father and mother, yes, that's what the fourth commandment says, but I can't love them." The more she thought about it, the sadder her heart grew. Isaiah says, "Though all forget thee, I thy God forget thee not. By thy name I have called thee, thou are mine." Faith was her only comfort, a straw to hold on to and her strength so that she did not yield to despair.

During the preparations before Christmas, she was distracted because of all the work that needed to be done and managed to blow the cobwebs away. Snow fell overnight and transformed nature into a fairy-tale landscape. Wistfulness rose in her and sadness settled around her soul.

She was unsuspecting until a letter from her grandmother reached her, telling her that her beloved grandfather had gone home. Now she understood her grief. He had thought of her even when he was dying, the grandmother wrote. And he still had a secret, he had taken it with him into eternity, where it would be safe. Amelie was inconsolable. Every evening she prayed and cried at the same time for her beloved grandfather, who was the only one who loved her.

It was no use, life went on. Warm rays of sunlight woke up the sleeping nature again. Amelie's heart also seemed to slowly overcome the grief for her beloved grandfather. How she would have loved to lay some more flowers on his grave, to thank him for everything. It was impossible, much too far away in Lower Styria, so all that remained was the loving memory of the loved one.

She still had to run errands for the family. Still lost in thought, she entered the bakery in the main street. Hermann came out of the next door with a loaf of bread in his arms. Full of joy, he called out to her: "Amelie! Is it really you?" "Yes, and you?" "The man from the summer party, remember? What about a quick cup of coffee together?" "With pleasure," she agreed, "I still have that much time, but then I have to go." "I've been thinking about you all the time these past few months." "Why is that?" she asked in surprise, sipping her coffee. She had never been in love and had never experienced nor thought it possible to please anyone. At that moment, something unprecedented stirred inside her that she didn't understand. "But now I have to go home in order to cook," she said softly. "May I see you again? Maybe on Sunday, when you're off? Just say yes." "Yes, let's say at 2:00 p.m. in front of the garden gate of the villa." Hermann was blissfully happy.

"Mother, mother!" he called out loudly when he returned home. "I have found her. Now I won't let her go. We'll meet again on Sunday afternoon." "Fine, then bring her for coffee."

Hermann could hardly wait for Sunday. His good mood was not to be overlooked and the work in the stable went as if by itself with so much joy. It would have been funny to know what his cows might have thought if they had been able to think. While ploughing and harrowing his fields, he could think of nothing else but Amelie. Now, at least, his work had a purpose.

Finally, the longed-for Sunday came. Amelie was already waiting at the gate of the villa and Hermann was on time. She couldn't understand why anyone was interested in her. She was just a maid. She had no idea that Hermann had fallen in love with her. He wanted to show her his home today and introduce her to his mother, who was already waiting for them with the table set and fragrant coffee.

The farm, just outside the village, bathing in spring sunshine, beamed at them. "This is my home, Amelie," at that, he looked at her lovingly, "and I would be happy if one day it would be yours, too." She did not know what to answer. His mother came out of the living room, happy to see them both.

Time flew by, the cows called loudly and Hermann had to go to the stable. "Shall I go with you?" Amelie asked. "I'd rather not. You won't get the stable perfume out of your beautiful hair so quickly. I'll hurry."

The two women talked about this and that as if they had known each other for a long time. The mother, beyond her prime, was well-groomed, well-dressed, her hair already greying and tied in a plait. Only her hands bore witness to much hard work. "No doubt, there's plenty of that."

Amelie was supposed to tell about herself, about her home and why she had left her homeland. "You really don't want to know, but some other time I'll be happy to tell you my story, though it's a very sad one." "Will you come again? I would be very happy if you did." "I think so if Hermann would like it." "You bet I would," echoed from the next room, where Hermann had showered and changed clothes.

The day was long gone. Countless stars glittered in the vault of the sky and the balmy spring wind brushed through the land. Hermann put his hand around her shoulder. "Will we meet again?" "If chance wants it again," she said softly and thought: I hope so. "Not by chance, I would prefer not to let you go. Can we meet again on Sunday? Please say yes, Amelie." "Yes, at the same time, in front of the gate." He would have liked to kiss her, but he was too slow.

In the evening, mother and son sat in their living room with a glass of red wine and let the day end. "Don't let go of that girl, you meet someone like that only once in a lifetime." "I would marry her on the spot, but I don't know if she wants me." "Then just ask her next Sunday," his mother advised.

Amelie's head was spinning, which was a feeling that she did not know. The mother was so loving and kind, which was something she had never known from her own mother. And Hermann was very reserved, obliging and kind. She sat in her room on the edge of her bed, thinking. "Have I fallen in love in the end? Well, it's possible, I'm old enough, after all."

The time until Sunday seemed like an eternity to her. She had pinned her hair up into a banana, powdered her cheeks a little and put on the most beautiful dress. She waited outside the gate. Hermann was on time as usual and without the famous scent. He was finely dressed up, as if he had planned something very special for today. "Wow, how pretty you are again today! I've been looking forward to this afternoon all week. And what about you? Did the week seem awfully long to you, too?" "An eternity," she answered shyly. He took her in his arms, hugged her tightly and kissed her on the cheek. "Oh, Amelie, how long I have waited for this moment, longing for you like a thirsty man for water." "Let's go," she begged. "Well, mother will be waiting, or do you have something against it?" "No, not at all, you have a loving mother, Hermann, we shouldn't keep her waiting."

Hermann's mother was eagerly waiting for them in the living room with coffee and a special bread called "Zopfbrot", as it was customary in this area. "I am very happy," said his mother in greeting, "that you have come again today. Oh, if only you could stay here forever," the old woman gushed. "How do you mean?" Amelie said while Hermann poured her coffee. "I am only a housekeeper, I have nothing and I am nothing. Moreover, a stranger among strangers. Sure, I've saved a little, but it's not much." "The more I get to know you, dear Amelie, I realise that you have more than gold and silver!" Hermann exclaimed to her, seeking her hand and holding it in his. "You have a good heart and two industrious hands. I have money of my own, but what use is all this to me without you?" He took a red rose from its hiding place, took her hand and asked firmly: "Amelie, will you marry me and stay here forever?" "Yes, Hermann." He kissed her on the mouth and she returned the kiss with passion. "At last I have a daughter!" the mother rejoiced. "I was so eagerly hoping that you would say yes and that we would become a family." "You are both so nice to me, but it's all happening too fast." "That's true," the mother said. "But I am no longer the youngest and Hermann has already passed 30. It's high time to start a family. Ever since he met you at the town festival, he's been a changed man. Amelie this, Amelie that. Thank the Lord that he found you again. You are grown-up people who are in the middle of life and know what you do and what you want." "Sure, that's true, but give me a little time to think." Amelie begged. Hermann still held her in his arms and did not want to let her go. He regretted that the cows had to be taken from the pasture to the barn for milking. "I would help you, but I don't have anything to wear for it." "Leave it, I have ordered Jakob for tonight. I'm sure he'll be here soon. Until I come back, you have some time to talk."

All too soon, that afternoon came to an end. Hermann wanted to call on her employers later in the week and ask them to cancel their employment contract so he could take her away as soon as possible. Amelie wrote to her pastor asking for his advice. The reply was brief. "Get married, be happy. You have my blessing."

It was the end of May. At that time, there was no opportunity for any romance on a farm. Everything had to be well thought out and planned. So Hermann asked his childhood friend, who had become a priest, to marry them in the nearby Lady Chapel. Amelie wrote to her parents and brother, asking them to come. The bride and groom did not want a special celebration, they were content with each other. Amelie was afraid because her life changed in a flash, almost like in a fairy tale. From a maid to a farmer's wife on a large farm. Hermann worried her. How should she behave? She had no experience with a man. But he was patient and could wait.

Everything was prepared for the big day. The house had been cleaned, the food had been ordered and the helpers had been assigned for the day. Her brother had already arrived. Her parents were not there and had not called in. There was little room in the chapel, but it was just right for the wedding ceremony in a small circle. Hermann wore a festive grey suit and

Amelie a white costume. She had a flower wreath in her hair and her wedding bouquet consisted of pink lilies and white freesias, her favourite flowers. The two promised to be faithful forever, in good times as well as in bad times, until death would part them. As a sign of their fidelity and attachment, the rings they put on each other's wedding finger were blessed. In a poem by Reinhard Johannes Sorge, it says: "We have promised each other / To salvation unbroken / For all eternity / We have found each other / Bound ourselves blood to blood / For all eternity. / No sword can separate us anymore / Because one thing was for both of us / For all eternity."

When the priest untied the white stole he had tied around her hands, Hermann was allowed to kiss his bride. His mother behind him wept for joy. The ceremony ended with the song: "Salve Regina".

In the inn, the table was festively laid for the small wedding party. They did not have much time to celebrate and even less time for a honeymoon. The hay harvest was just around the corner. Only this one day belonged to them and no one was to take away their joy. In the pile of letters on the desk, Amelie found a letter from her mother. "How can you do this to me, marrying a German! We're not coming." She had to sit down. What was that supposed to mean? Holding the letter in her hands, she started to cry. "What happened?" Hermann asked, embracing her and pressing her against him. "Don't cry!" „She doesn't even wish me happiness!" "Who is 'she'?" "My mother." "But why?" "I have no idea." "Come on, let us toast this special day and thank our Creator that we have found each other."

The lights were out, only the moon witnessed their devotion and love. Hermann showered her with kisses and she returned his passion. When the moon had long since gone to sleep, they fell asleep, close together.

Early in the morning at sunrise, the young woman stretched out her left arm, still half asleep, groping for Hermann. But the bed was empty. A glance at the clock showed that she had overslept. Quietly, the door opened and Hermann came to the bed to wake her. She pulled him to her. "You slept so sweetly, I didn't want to wake you after such a beautiful night." "Now I'll make breakfast for everyone," Amelie said.

She quickly went to take a shower and then marched to the kitchen. The smell of freshly brewed coffee already met her in the hallway. In the dining area, the mother was waiting at the beautifully set breakfast table. "Come on, children, let's have breakfast and afterwards we have some things to discuss. Now, how was the wedding night?" she asked and looked at Hermann. "Wonderful, mother, just beautiful." "Well, then everything is fine. Remember that I want to become a grandmother before the Lord takes me away. And since we're already on the subject: When I was in your place, I swore this to myself: If ever I will have a daughter-in-law, I will be a mother to her, not a mother-in-law. For I could not please my mother-in-law at that time. Everything had to go the way she wanted. From now on, my dear Amelie, I have a daughter in addition to my son. You are the new farmer's wife and I can retire." "Out of the question, mother, you will remain in our midst. We need you, only you won't be allowed to work so much anymore." "You're just too good, Amelie. Many young women send old people to the old folks' home or to the old people's home." "Out of the question," Hermann intervened, holding his wife's hand. „Here are all the keys of the house and here is the purse. I don't want," the mother emphasised, „that you always have to ask whether you can buy this or that. I have seen how thrifty you are with money and how you turn over every note twice. When everything is used up, you withdraw money from the bank. I appeal to you, Hermann, that both of you are registered at the bank. A power of attorney alone is not enough. You never know what may be waiting for you. I have learned from my experience. Now, I hope we have discussed the important things." "Just one more thing," Hermann spoke up and took his wife's hand firmly in his. "I beg you to take driving lessons." "But how on earth shall I get that, my dear? I'm a technical idiot and much too stupid for that." "That's what they put you up to. But this is not true, Amelie. You can do so many things, I'm proud of you. My schoolmate has a driving school. I'll give him a call." "But that costs money." "Didn't you hear my mother's words? What has to be, has to be. Of course, I will help you. You have to be independent. As soon as you have passed the exam, we'll buy a used car just for you." "That's nice, Hermann," his mother said, smiling at him. "You are supposed to finally be happy, Amelie, and to forget the bad times you have endured."

If only it were that simple. The hay harvest was coming up. "The weather forecast is good, we can venture." Amelie contradicted her husband: "It will rain in a short time, look, the dawn and no morning dew. The swallows fly low, too. My grandfather has always followed the events of nature and has almost always been right. The sun is at its zenith, heating up mightily. The hay will dry quickly, we have to start immediately so that some of it gets under the roof." Hermann agreed and already in the afternoon the first grass fell. The next day they were able to bale the dry hay. Dark clouds appeared in the sky, not promising anything good. Thick raindrops pelted the earth. "Good thing I listened to my wife," Hermann said delightedly and Jakob could only confirm it. "At least, we have mown down part of it and the rain will allow new grass to grow."

On Sunday, the two lovers practised driving in the yard. Starting, accelerating and braking. It worked. They were happy. Amelie found out that she was not stupid as she had always been told. She passed the driving test. They went to the car dealer and bought a second-hand Polo. He had promised her, after all. Never in her dreams would she have thought of having her own car. She wanted to thank her husband, but he waved her off. "What is mine is yours. I want you to be just as happy as I am."

The grain in the fields shone golden yellow. The sun was heating mightily in these so-called dog days. Hermann and Jakob prepared the harvesting machine and the transporter. First the moisture had to be measured. If it was too high, the grain had to go to the drying plant and that would be expensive. Everything was in order. First the brewing barley was harvested and sold to the brewery. Then came the wheat. As soon as the sun dried the dew in the early morning, the men set to work. Hermann was at the threshing machine, Jakob came with the truck. A second helper was also present today with his truck so that the grain could be transported quickly to the hall. Amelie brought lunch and drinks to the men in a basket. Time was rushing. A thunderstorm was forecast for the night and they still had a few acres to mow. They wouldn't get it all done today, tomorrow was another day. Amelie had to get the cows from the pasture. They were already waiting at the gate, restless and in need of milking. She opened the gate and the cows followed the lead cow one by one into the barn. Each one went to her place. Now Amelie had to throw in some dry feed and then it was time for milking. Finally she fed the calves in their stalls. A lot of work for a woman. But she loved this work, which had accompanied her for as long as she could remember. Her husband could rely on her. Dog-tired, they fell into their beds around midnight. The alarm clock rang again at 5:00 a.m. Together they went to the stable. They had to go fast today. The day was tightly planned. Every hour counted. The remaining wheat had to be threshed and brought into the hall before the weather changed. Straw also had to be baled and made ready for collection at the edge of the field. When they brought the last load into the hall, Petrus opened the floodgates and it poured with rain. "Thank the Lord!" Hermann exclaimed. "We made it!"

Meanwhile, the mother had prepared a snack for the hungry workers. Hermann and Jakob ate their fill, only Amelie couldn't get a bite down. "I don't feel well today," she said, drank some water and went to bed. The Mother said quietly, "Well, maybe I will become a grandmother, after all. She works too much," she admonished her son. "She needs to get more rest." "You are right, mother, we'll talk about it tomorrow."

The cows had been milked, the milk was ready. Punctually as always, at 7 o'clock, the milk truck came to collect the precious cargo. At breakfast, Hermann quickly skimmed through the newspaper, annoyed by what was written there, grumbling about politics. The milk price had dropped again. "We farmers are the stupidest under the sun, slaving day in and day out so that the population has enough to eat, having no holiday except for the few hours on Sunday afternoon." Angrily, he left the house and went to the field. He wanted to plough up today and sow green manure. Above all, he wanted to get rid of his anger. It was not easy for him. He had studied agricultural science, taken over the farm from his father and brought everything up to date. Together with other farmers, he had set up a fleet of machines, counting on the income from the daily milk production of his 80 cows.

Amelie had never seen him so angry. She just shook her head as she coated the roast pork with mustard, seared it, put it in the roasting tin with herbs and root vegetables, poured broth and red wine over it and put it in the oven. As she did so, she was surprised by a sharp, burning pain in her abdomen. At the same moment she saw the blood under her Bermuda shorts already dripping onto the floor. Her mother-in-law was busy peeling potatoes, but reacted with presence of mind, laid her daughter-in-law on the floor, padded her abdomen with towels and called the ambulance. "Lie very still and keep your legs together tightly!" She put another chair cushion under her head.

The paramedics and the emergency doctor were on the spot. The situation was clear. They carefully placed Amelie on the stretcher and took her into the ambulance. She was given fresh bandages and an infusion and was taken to the hospital by the lake with blue lights. The emergency doctor informed his colleagues. They had to hurry, the blood loss was enormous and the blood pressure was low. The operation was prepared. They put the patient on the operating table. Luckily, she had not been able to eat anything in the morning, so the anaesthetist could start with the short anaesthesia. Everything had to be done quickly so that she would not lose even more blood. The uterus had to be scraped out, because that was the only way the gynaecologist could stop the bleeding. "I guess," the doctor said, "you were in the 12th week. The bleeding must continuously be monitored. Another infusion please and labs." She was placed in a hospital bed and taken to the ward. The doctor gave some more orders.

Hermann, who had been notified by his mother in the meantime, could not believe what had happened. He was already waiting in the long corridor. He couldn't stand it to sit still on the chair, so he was pacing up and down. Finally the nurses brought his wife, who was still fast asleep. "How is she?" he asked anxiously. "Are you the husband? Yes? All right, then come with me." "May I stay with her until she wakes up?" "Sure," the nurse replied. She placed a chair next to Amelie's bed, admonishing him to ring the bell as soon as his wife would wake up.

After an hour, she slowly woke up. The nurse checked the vital signs and the drapes. The blood counts were also ready.

The bleeding stopped. The doctor came to check on her. "Are you the husband?" "Yes. What happened to my wife?" "She had a miscarriage with heavy bleeding. It's good that your mother reacted so quickly, otherwise she would have bled to death. She needs a lot of rest now. Tomorrow you can take your wife home if the blood values are OK, but only after the round, let's say around 10 o'clock." "Good," Hermann said and thanked the doctor. "Thank your mother for the quick help. She would have bled to death otherwise."

The next day Amelie sat on her bed, waiting for Hermann. The doctor came for his rounds and inquired about her condition. Hermann had also arrived in the meantime. "I see," the doctor said, "you are already feeling better. Unfortunately, I still have to tell you something." They both stared at the doctor. "Do you want to have children?" They had not expected this question. "Yes, sure," they both answered at the same time. "Sure, you will be able to get pregnant again, but you won't be able to carry a child to full term because your uterus is, so to say, not in the right position. Did you have to work hard when you were a child?" "Ever since I can remember," Amelie replied. "And what do the welts on your back and thighs mean?" "They are sad reminders of times gone by." "Well, with a little surgery we can fix the problem by putting the uterus in its intended place and stitching it up. Come to my office in a fortnight. Until then, relaxation and absolute bed rest are the orders of the day. Even working in the stable is taboo for you until then because germs are lurking everywhere and you are not up to it yet. I wish you both all the best and see you in a fortnight," the doctor said goodbye.

The mother-in-law had already prepared dinner and was waiting for them in the dining area. She had cooked a hearty broth for Amelie. "This will do you good," she said. Then she told them about herself. She had experienced the same thing and could therefore sympathise with her daughter-in-law.

After a detailed consultation, Amelie was operated on. However, it would take some time for everything to heal and to be ready for another pregnancy for her. "Never again will I leave the house angry," Hermann said one evening as they were all sitting together and having a glass of wine. "I got horribly angry that morning about the falling price of milk, and the politics to go with it. I beg your pardon, my dear. It doesn't bear contemplating if I had lost you that very day." "Long forgotten," Amelie said, "but you still carry it around with you. Gone is gone. We all have bad days." With that she stroked his cheek and looked at him lovingly with her blue eyes.

The work in the fields was done, the garden tidied up. The cows had left their pasture for a few months and were in the barn with hay and silage. Autumn with its colourful splendour had long since taken its leave. Fog shrouded the fields and the cold east wind did not bode well. Winter was not far away. Hermann sat in his office, planning and calculating for the coming year. The full manure barrel worried him. He was supposed to spread the stinking waste, but the weather did not allow it. Fortunately, he still had half a storage room capacity. The spreading of slurry was limited and forbidden on penalty when the ground was wet and frozen. Furthermore, he had to pay attention to the crop rotation for the coming year so that he could get another good harvest. He added up the expenses and compared them with the income. Tax and insurance were also added. He was not enthusiastic about this bureaucratic work, yet it was important.

A surprise phone call from Amelie's father brought nothing good. Mother had died and the funeral was in three days. Amelie didn't know what to do, but Hermann said: "No matter what she did to you, she is your mother and we will accompany her on her last journey. I'll discuss everything with Jakob and mother, then I'll order a wreath and we'll go."

It was a long way to Lower Styria. In Austria, the snow-covered mountains greeted with their illuminated churches and chapels. Fortunately, the motorway was free, so they reached their destination after ten hours.

A large crowd was already gathered in the cemetery hall. Amelie felt lost. She had not seen her mother for years. Her heart raced as she stepped up to the bier. There lay the woman who had given her life but had never loved her. Her expression was bitter, her hair greying, her worn hands folded in prayer. Amelie trembled as she used to do when she met her father. But now Hermann was with her and held her hand. Some women prayed the rosary. Then the coffin was closed and taken to the church for the funeral mass. After that it was taken in procession to the grave. The pallbearers slowly lowered the coffin into the dark grave while the priest prayed. Amelie cried continuously and wished her mother peace and eternal rest. Her father took her aside and shouted at her: "You don't have to cry! I shall tell you from your mother it's your fault that she had to die." Those present fell silent. Hermann took his wife tightly in his arms and brought her to the car. He put her in the passenger seat, fastened the seat belt and drove off.

Amelie cried heartbreakingly. "Why is it my fault? She died of cancer, didn't she? They say she said goodbye to everyone, but she didn't want to see me. Why, Hermann, why?" Only when they reached the Karawanken Tunnel, which connects Slovenia and Austria, did the pain and grief subside. Both were tired and exhausted. In Spital an der Drau they found a hotel, could stay overnight and got something to eat.

Finally they were back home. Hermann told his mother about the sad things they had experienced. She could not believe that a child was blamed for the death of its mother. She took Amelie in her arms, stroked her pale cheeks and comforted her. "Maybe one day you will find out why. People say that time heals all wounds, but they forget that scars remain."

At last it was Christmas Eve. In the living room, Amelie had decorated the Christmas tree with red baubles and a string of lights. The table was finely set. As usual, there was potato salad with Vienna sausages, bread and punch on Christmas Eve. Christmas carols sounded from the radio and the ringing of the bells could be heard from the nearby church. Hermann read the Christmas story. Afterwards, they prayed the Lord's Prayer together, including the living and the deceased. "I never had such a nice Christmas Eve when I was a child," Amelie said. "There were always arguments about something I never understood. And there weren't any presents."

Over a glass of punch and biscuits they had baked at the beginning of Advent they wished each other a blessed Christmas. Amelie held her husband's hand tightly, looking at him lovingly with her blue eyes. Then she said bluntly: "We are going to have a child." Mother and son were overwhelmed. Hermann embraced his wife, kissed her full of joy, but the mother worried if everything would go well this time. "There is one catch," Amelie continued. „I'm not allowed to work much anymore. I have to go to the doctor's office every month." „Don't worry, my darling. As soon as the holidays are over, I'll start looking for a suitable helper. In the meantime, mother will look after you so that you can take it easy." "I'm not made of cotton wool and pregnancy is a normal thing." "That's true, but I don't want to relive the past," the father-to-be responded with concern.

Snow had fallen overnight, turning nature into a fairy-tale landscape. The Rough Nights begin on Christmas Day and end on Epiphany. These twelve days prophesy the weather of the new year. The so-called "Lostage" were not always accurate, but they were helpful. Each day represents a month. "Grandfather," remembered Amelie, "always wrote them down and treasured these days." She had sprinkled the farm with Epiphany water and mixed the consecrated salt into the cows' feed. This was an old custom from her homeland.

Winter had them all firmly in its grip. Every now and then the sun peeked out from behind a cloud and made the yellow flowering mustard fields shine in all their splendour in the middle of winter. Ice crystals clung to their leaves, but the flowers stretched out towards the sun. The local birds, blackbirds, robins, tits and sparrows, were constantly foraging. A pair of pigeons cooed on the roof of the house and diligently visited the full bird house, which Amelie refilled with food.

Slowly, she felt the movements of her child. At the last check-up and ultrasound everything was fine. „Congratulations, you are expecting a son," the gynaecologist announced. Rest was still the order of the day. "Don't forget to drink. Water, of course. — And how are you managing at home?" the friendly doctor wanted to know. "Fine, my husband has hired a helper for this time so I can take it easy." "Fine, then we'll see each other again in a month."

Beaming with joy, she announced to her husband, "We are having a son!" He was beside himself with joy, took her in his arms and kissed her. A little later he presented her with a bouquet of flowers. The mother-in-law was also happy about the news but was still very worried.

Slowly, snowdrops stretched their white heads out of the ground and winter bulbs held their yellow blossoms out to the industrious and hungry insects. No doubt, spring was approaching with great strides. Once again the sequence of agricultural work began: ploughing, harrowing, sowing and much else. "I don't know whether I'm coming or going," Hermann complained. "Cow after cow is calving in the next few days." Good thing he had still hired Oliver for the coming months. With 80 cows, there was a lot of work and responsibility. Almost nothing was earned in the process. Before giving birth, the cow is drained, which means she is not milked, and after calving the calves are given so-called "Biestmilch" (beest milk) for one to two weeks. After that they are fed with milk powder unless they are sold at a price of between 10 and 20 euros. In contrast, 1 kilogram of veal costs at least 15 euros in the butcher's shop. Some calves are also traded by price per kilo, depending on the breed.

Amelie loved this work, but now she had to stay away and was only allowed to watch. Hermann was very strict with her in this respect. He comforted her, stroked her belly and felt the movements of the unborn. "Maybe he'll be a football player, being a farmer isn't necessarily rewarding, but it's nice for me anyway. If only it weren't for all this bureaucracy."

In the meantime, spring had come into the country with all its splendour. Behind the house, the sweet cherry blossomed, wrapped in its white flower dress, competing with the peach tree in the garden with its pink blossoms. Bees flew from blossom to blossom, collecting nectar and pollinating the flowers. The wagtail was also back from the south, proudly strolling around the garden, looking for insects. „Grandfather loved this bird," Amelie recalled, "it is proof of the eagerly awaited spring."

Now it was time to furnish the nursery. The wicker cot, where Hermann once lay, was furnished with new fabric. Above it, the canopy was stretched with white lace. They had bought a new changing table, baby scales, nappies, everything for the first weeks. The pram was also ready in the corner. "You never know if the baby is in a hurry to come into the world or if he is taking his time," Amelie said. "They say girls hurry, whereas boys take their time." A strange feeling beset her, accompanied by fear. "Will everything be all right?" she asked herself. The unborn baby was kicking in her belly and everything was fine. Those were the reassuring words of the doctor at the last check-up. "Four more weeks, my little one," she said as she lovingly stroked and creamed her belly. One more visit to the doctor, then it would be time.

In the meantime, Hermann and his helpers had a lot of work to do in the fields, the hay harvest was coming up soon. The potato fields were tilled, the maize and turnips sown. This year he had also thought of the bees and planted flower seeds along the edges of the fields. The weather was favourable, it was sunny and it was supposed to be hot, just right for the first grass cutting.

Over breakfast, they discussed the day's work. Together with Oliver and Jakob, they mounted the cutter bars on the tractor. Amelie waved at them before getting into her polo. They waved back.

The last check-up before the birth in four weeks was due today. It wasn't far to town and she drove carefully. A BMW driver came speeding up from behind, touched the little Polo, ripped off the wing mirror in the process and drove off. Amelie was very frightened, left the road and landed in the ditch. She hit her head on the steering wheel and lost consciousness. Oncoming motorists immediately informed the police and paramedics. The emergency doctor informed the nearby hospital after they had carefully freed the heavily pregnant woman from the wreckage. They drove away with flashing blue lights. She was in a critical condition, still unconscious. At the hospital she was examined and the doctors checked the heart tones of the unborn child. They were weak and the injured woman was still far away.

Hermann was on his way to lunch with his helpers and had to pass the accident site. He dismounted to get to the car, which was being transported to the tow truck. A policeman stopped him. "My God!" he shouted loudly. "That's my wife's car. What about her? Where is she? She's heavily pregnant!" "She is in the hospital," the policeman reassured him.

Hermann hurried home. Fear for his wife choked his throat, he couldn't eat. Everyone was deeply shaken. He gave instructions to his helpers, changed his clothes and drove to his beloved wife in the hospital. Mother lit a candle in the corner of the sanctuary, folded her hands and prayed.

Meanwhile, the doctors had decided to perform an emergency caesarean section. They wanted to save both the mother and her child. Everyone was ready. The anaesthetist had a big responsibility. He reported, "We can start." After three minutes Nico saw the light of day. The child had apparently not been affected by anything. It was healthy and quite strong for its 8 months; nevertheless, the time was inconvenient. In the adjoining room, he was cared for by the paediatrician and by the midwife. "Now we can turn to the mother." The assistant doctor first sewed up the caesarean wound, then the gaping wound above the temple. A nurse applied bandages and changed the dressings of the still sleeping patient. The vital signs were checked on a monitor and infusions were changed in the arm. The lab technician took blood for the examination. The head had to be x-rayed. To all appearances, there were no fractures. "She was really lucky. She must have had several guardian angels," the doctor pointed out. "It is a mystery to me why she hasn't woken up yet. To be sure, we'll notify our neurologist."

Hermann paced up and down the corridor. He couldn't think in a straight way. He was full of fear for his wife and wondered what was wrong with the child. A nurse led him to Amelie. "The doctor is still with her, checking the equipment. Are you the husband?" "Yes, Schwarz is my name." Then he cried out loud: "Amelie!" and kissed her cheek. As he did so, his tears wet her pale sunken face. "Will she wake up again?" "Sure," the doctor reassured him. "And what about the child?" he asked further. "We had to perform an emergency caesarean section. You have a healthy son. Congratulations." The present nurse pushed a light brown padded chair to the sick woman's bedside. "Sit down, it might last a while until she wakes up." The midwife brought the newborn lying in a pillow into the room.

How much he had been looking forward to this moment! Now he felt like crying. A child without a mother, unthinkable. Tormented by doubts and torn apart inside, he could not hold back his tears. He had no more hope. Manfred, his friend, the priest, came just at the right moment. "Hermann, what has happened? Your mother called me." "A car accident, look, she won't wake up." "And your child, whom you were so eagerly looking forward to?" "They had to come and get it. It's a healthy boy." "I don't know you like this, Hermann, so desperate and despondent. Believe and trust in God's help. She will wake up again. If you allow me, I will give her the anointing of the sick." "Last rites, you mean?" "No, my friend, she should not die, but wake up and live. You do not understand me. Anointing of the sick is not a ladder to heaven at the last moment of our lives, but loving attention from God in sickness and distress. It helps her to get well and to get through the tragic."

The priest prayed and Hermann responded. Then he anointed her forehead and hands with the oil for the sick. He said: "Through this holy anointing, may the Lord help you in his abundant mercy, may he assist you with the power of the Holy Spirit. May the Lord, who frees you from sins, save you and raise you up in his grace. Amen." Together they prayed the Lord's Prayer. With the blessing of the sick, Manfred said goodbye and promised to come again.

In the meantime it had become evening. Darkness spread. In the light of the street lamp and the burning candle on the table, Hermann looked at his wife, who was still sleeping, holding her hand. Suddenly he felt a slight movement of her fingers. For a moment, she opened her eyes, groped over her somewhat flattened belly, in which she

94

felt no life but only the bandage on her lower abdomen. "My child, where is my child?" she asked softly, fainting again.

The doctor, the nurses and the midwife rushed in. They wanted to move the sick woman and take care of her. They asked Hermann to go home, rest and come back the next day. Reluctantly, he did as he was bid.

At home he told his waiting mother what had happened and that they had a son. Then he burst into tears. The believing woman took her son in her arms and comforted him. He was completely exhausted and tired, nevertheless, he was unable to sleep. Countless stars were shining in the sky, foretelling beautiful weather. His interest was only in his wife now. All the work was done by helpers. He knew he could rely on them.

After a short sleepless night, he hurried back to the hospital. He wanted to be there when she woke up. So he sat waiting by her bedside again. The children's nurse brought the little one back into the room, put the child in the mother's arms, waiting to see what would happen. The child began to cry, the mother opened her eyes, looked around and asked: "Where am I?" "In the hospital," Hermann said. Only now did she notice her crying child. "Our son," Hermann said, but she was much too weak to respond. The nurse took the little one away again. She had achieved what she had read in a magazine. The child's cry had woken the mother. Hermann held her hand. He wept for joy. The doctor, the nurses and the midwife rejoiced with him. Manfred also came by again. He had thought deeply of Amelie during the service and prayed for her. Then there was a knock at the door. The police asked how the victims were doing. At the same time, they reported that they had the person who had caused the accident. A young man had overtaken other cars with his BMW, underestimated the speed and ended up on the tree. He was dead. "The car is not a toy and the road is not a race track," the police officer stressed. "Innocent people die, families break apart, grief and pain remain. You almost got hit, too. Continue to get well, the insurance will take care of the rest."

Amelie couldn't believe she had slept that long. She was still very weak, but she tried to breastfeed her child with the help of the children's nurse. Hermann could not believe his regained happiness. He wanted to hold on to it and was grateful to Manfred for his support and prayers. He ordered a bouquet of Amelie's favourite flowers, roses and freesias for his wife. She still had to stay in the hospital, get her strength back and undergo further examinations. Only when she was completely recovered was she allowed to go home. She could already try the first steps in her room. It worked. Only her circulation was on strike. She still needed a lot of rest.

Meanwhile, Hermann had a lot of work in the field. A lot had been left undone and now had to be caught up. Together with Jakob and Oliver, he brought the hay bales home and stacked them near the stable. A winter supply for his animals. The flower meadow by his cornfields shone. There were light blue cornflowers and red poppies, in between white daisies stretched their heads towards the sun. Countless insects were enjoying the splendour of the blossoms. Despite all the work, Hermann visited his wife. The injury on her forehead and the caesarean scar had healed, the stitches had been removed. She was stable again and was soon allowed to go home with her child. However, her joy was subdued. She had dreamed all sorts of things during the long sleep, remembering them only incompletely. She had asked her mother "Why?" and had got no answer. After all, it was only a dream that wouldn't let her go. When she was small, someone had once told her, that she would not resemble her father and would only have a few of her mother's features. She did not understand what that meant. Only one thing was clear to her today, she had been unloved and had always been in the way. She was still waiting for an answer. One thing was also clear to her, if the Creator had wanted it differently, she would not be alive. What horrible thoughts! Fortunately, the sister just brought the little one to get nursed, thus distracting her.

At home, everything was prepared for her return. The mother had cooked with the helper, the table was set. Finally, joy had dispelled the sorrow and life returned to the farm. The sun heated up mightily, letting the grain ripen and vegetables grow. From time to time, Petrus opened his floodgates and the rain soaked the thirsty nature. Only the fear of a thunderstorm, which often brought hail, was great so close to the harvest. The happy grandma walked around the yard with her grandson, who slept contentedly in his light grey pram. She had never thought she would live to see this. With the hard work on the farm and increasing age, her strength was waning. Amelie looked after her lovingly, showed her respect and gratitude. Nico kicked in the pram and smiled at her just like his father once did.

Actually, the grain harvest did come again. The combine harvester was ready, along with a truck and a trailer. The weather seemed to hold according to the forecast, but Amelie was sceptical. Early in the morning, the dawn beamed at her. There was no morning dew but an eerie silence instead. Not a single bird flew by or chirped.

"Hurry up," she called to the men, "there will be a thunderstorm!" The farmer is dependent on the weather, on the whim of nature, on many regulations of politics and, ultimately, on the financial market strategy. He has to sell his products cheaply, on which the trade earns its golden nose. An example of this is calves and milk. The consumer has to dig deep into his pocket for those products. So it's no wonder that farms are dying. Hermann calculated: Had the modern barn been worth it? Could he pay off the loan with the sale of his products? He was also concerned about animal welfare. "As long as the animals live with me, they should have a good life. Ultimately, they become our food." Yet he wanted to continue doing his job; actually, he could not imagine a more beautiful profession, even if, on some days, he felt like smashing his rubber boots dripping with dirt into the corner along with the stinking filthy stable clothes. But without the agricultural perfume, there would be neither milk nor bread. His family gave him strength every day.

Actually, Amelie had every reason to be glad and happy. She had survived everything and could cheerfully watch her son grow up. Nico had meanwhile become a little sunshine for the whole family and one thing was already obvious: he loved animals.

The fields had now been harvested, the manure spread and ploughed under. The cattle were back in the barn. The circle of agricultural work was closed again and the autumnal mist threw its grey mantle over all nature and let it rest. Despite all the happiness Amelie experienced with the family, deep sadness sometimes overcame her. She asked herself why she should be to blame for her mother's death. This question remained unanswered until the day when a letter from her father stuck out from under the pile of the day's mail. Amelie did not dare to open it, but Hermann wanted to read it. Unfortunately, he did not speak Slovenian, so his wife had to translate word for word. Once again, she experienced all the drama and pain of her childhood. Her father wrote what had happened during that terrible night in the camp in the summer of 1945:

"Then your mother became pregnant with you. To spare her the shame, as she called it, we got married. Love was not involved. I have regretted it all my life. For her, physical love was dirty and without any pleasure, even less joy. She worked all day, her mind completely elsewhere. In recent years, she often sat on the banks of the Saddle Brook, staring into the river. She was mentally absent. The family doctor feared suicide. Together we considered whether it would not be better to admit her to a psychiatric clinic near the district town. To make matters worse, she complained of stomach pains. On some days she could eat everything, on others she even vomited her tea. After much toing and froing, she was referred to the district hospital for a gastroscopy. Stomach cancer had long since spread and had her firmly in its grip. She was not even allowed to go home since she was immediately prepared for an operation. The doctors intended to perform a gastric resection according to Billroth II. This involves removing the stomach, creating a new small stomach from the small intestine (jejunum) and connecting it to the oesophagus. There were complications that night. An internal haemorrhage allegedly occurred and there had to be another operation. I did not find out any more details. Death lurked in the corridors of the hospital, waiting for his cue. That night he was ordered to fetch your mother. She had longed for him, but did not wake up from the anaesthetic. So he carried her asleep into another world, awaited with longing. You have suffered greatly from everything, my dear Amelie. I have not been as kind to you as I should have been. Please forgive me. Please,

Amelie, I only have about three months to live. I've been struck by a rare kind of leukaemia with no hope of recovery."

"This is hardly surprising: a nuclear reactor is only 25 kilometres away as the crow flies. All his relatives died of some kind of cancer," Amelie said. Hermann moved his chair close to Amelie, holding her tightly. "Will you be able to forgive him?" "Yes," she said, "I have to, so he can go in peace. But I can't forget. The scars on my back and thighs always remind me." Now her tears were unstoppable. Nico, who had been playing with Lego bricks in his play corner the whole time, climbed onto his mother's lap. He held her tightly with his delicate hands and gave her a big kiss: "Don't cry, Mummy, I'm with you after all."